Blue & Pink
Balloons

This is my mommy and daddy. We love to play, be silly, and snuggle.

I love them so much!

This is me. My name is Sadie and I am 4 years old.

I love pretending and going to ballet and tap class.

I go to preschool and love
playing with my friends.

School is fun and I am learning so much.

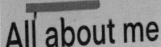
All about me

Some have both.

Some of my friends have sisters or brothers.

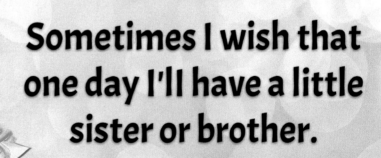

Sometimes I wish that one day I'll have a little sister or brother.

We would giggle,
play games, and
pretend.

We would always be there for each other.

Today Mommy and Daddy told me they have a surprise. I wonder what it could be.

We sit down on the couch.
Mommy is holding balloons that are
blue and pink.

Daddy says, "We have exciting news to share, sweetie. There is a baby in Mommy's belly!" My wish had finally come true!

I jump up and down so excited and yell,
"I get to be a big sister!"

I will teach the baby all I know. Like walking, playing hide and seek, and how to color.

Weeks go by and today is special. Mommy and Daddy are going to the doctor while I'm at preschool.

When they pick me up, they said they will have a picture of my baby sister or brother. It is called an ultrasound.

School was so much fun.
Today we painted outside.

My favorite part was playing on the swings.

It's time to go home...
Oh, I can't wait! We all
lined up outside. I see my
mommy and daddy
waiting for me.

It's my turn to go, so I run to them as fast as I can. I can't wait to see the picture of the baby!

At home, we sit down on the couch. Daddy is holding balloons that are blue and pink. He says, "Sweetie, we have to talk," and Mommy wipes her eyes with a tissue. I wonder why she is sad.

"The baby that was in Mommy's belly was sick and it had to go back to heaven."
"So I don't get to be a big sister?" I asked confused.
Daddy said, "Not for now, honey. We're so sorry!"

This made me sad and I wanted to cry. I really want to be a big sister! Mommy and Daddy give me a big hug and say, "It's okay to feel sad."

"You may not be able to see the baby in person, but now you will have a guardian angel, and you can talk to the baby whenever you want to or when you pray."

"Can we do something special for the baby?" I ask. "Of course we can" Mommy says. "What if we tie one of the baby's pictures to the balloons and fly them up to heaven?" Daddy asks.

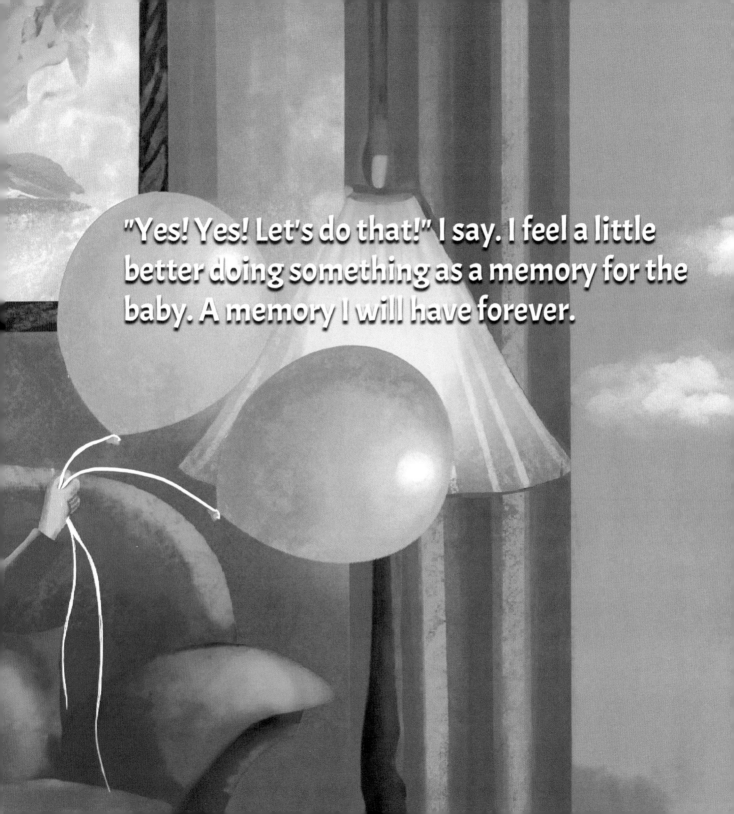

"Yes! Yes! Let's do that!" I say. I feel a little better doing something as a memory for the baby. A memory I will have forever.

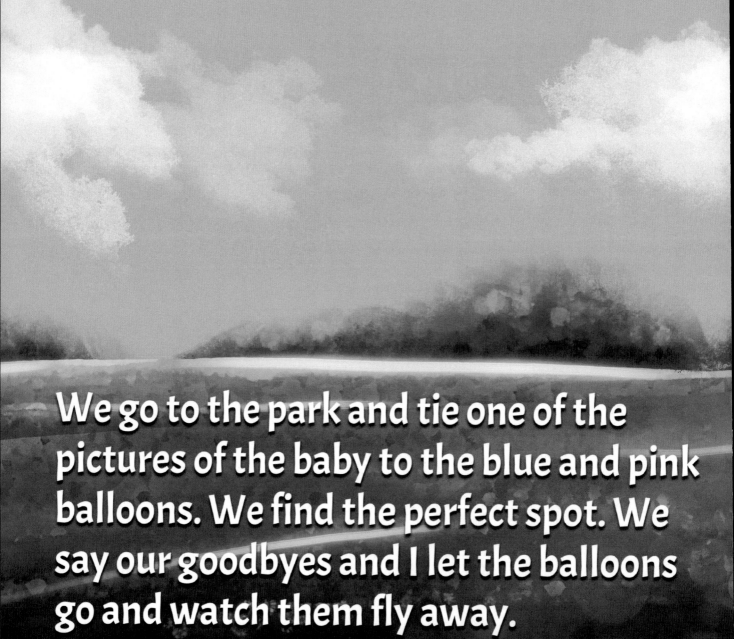

We go to the park and tie one of the pictures of the baby to the blue and pink balloons. We find the perfect spot. We say our goodbyes and I let the balloons go and watch them fly away.

I will always be a big sister in my heart, and I have my very own angel to talk to, but sometimes I feel sad and that's okay.

Maybe one day I will have a little brother or little sister.

Maybe I won't. I do know that whatever happens, my mommy and daddy will love me all the time, every day, no matter what!

This is an actual photo of the author's daughter Sadie releasing the blue and pink balloons into the sky the day they learned of the miscarriage.

Made in the USA
Las Vegas, NV
17 April 2024

88759353R20021